Uncle Russ and the Letter **U**

Alphabet Friends

by Cynthia Klingel and Robert B. Noyed

The Child's World®

The Child's World

Published in the United States of America
by The Child's World®
P.O. Box 326
Chanhassen, MN 55317-0326
800-599-READ
www.childsworld.com

The Child's World®: Mary Berendes, Publishing Director

Editorial Directions, Inc.: E. Russell Primm, Editorial
Director; Emily Dolbear, Line Editor; Ruth Martin,
Editorial Assistant; Linda S. Koutris, Photo Researcher
and Selector

Photographs ©: BananaStock/Punchstock: Cover & 20;
William James Warren/Corbis: 11; Digital Vision/Getty
Images: 12; IT Stock Free/Creatas: 15; Stockbyte/
Creatas: 16; Brand X Pictures/Punchstock: 19.

Library of Congress Cataloging-in-Publication Data
Klingel, Cynthia Fitterer.
  Uncle Russ and the letter U / by Cynthia Klingel and
Robert B. Noyed.
    p. cm. — (Alphabet readers)
Summary: A simple story about a boy named Ulysses
and his silly Uncle Russ introduce the letter "u".
  ISBN 1-59296-111-8 (Library Bound : alk. paper)
  [1. Uncles—Fiction. 2. Alphabet.] I. Noyed, Robert B.,
ill. II. Title. III. Series.
  PZ7.K6798Un 2003
  [E]—dc21
                                    2003006614

Note to parents and educators:

The first skill children acquire before becoming successful readers is individual letter recognition. The Alphabet Friends series has been created with the needs of young learners in mind. Each engaging book begins by showing the difference between the capital letter and the lowercase letter. In each of the books on the vowels and the consonants c and g, children are introduced to the different sounds that the letter can make. Finally, children see that the letters can be found at the beginning of a word, in the middle of a word, and in most cases, at the end of a word.

Following the introduction, children meet their Alphabet Friends. The friend in each story encounters many words that include the featured letter of that book. Each noun that begins with the title letter is highlighted in red with the initial letter of the word in bold. Above the word is a rebus drawing that establishes a strong picture cue.

At the end of each book, we have included three words lists. Can your young learners find all the words in each book with the title letter in them?

Let's learn about the letter **U.**

The letter **U** can look like this: **U.**

The letter **U** can also look like this: **u.**

The letter **u** makes two different sounds.

One sound is the long sound,

like in the word uniform.

uniform

The other sound is the short sound,

like in the word umbrella.

umbrella

The letter **u** can be at the
beginning of a word, like uncle.

uncle

The letter **u** can be in the
middle of a word, like house.

ho**u**se

The letter **u** can be at the
end of a word, like tutu.

tut**u**

It was an ugly day outside. Rain drummed

on the window. **U**ncle Russ needed to

get up.

Suddenly **U**ncle Russ heard a loud

sound. **U**lysses came running upstairs

in his school **u**niform. "Get up,

Uncle Russ!"

Uncle Russ jumped out from under the

covers. **U**lysses chuckled. **U**ncle Russ was

a funny guy.

Ulysses told **U**ncle Russ that it was

time to leave. **U**lysses went to get his

backpack and **u**mbrella. He waited

for **U**ncle Russ.

Ulysses went out the door. He opened up

his **u**mbrella. He stood under the **u**mbrella

to keep his **u**niform dry. **U**lysses was

unsure when **U**ncle Russ was coming.

Ulysses went up the steps to find

Uncle Russ. He could not believe

what he saw. "Get up, **U**ncle Russ!

It's time to walk me to school."

Fun Facts

What do nurses, soldiers, police officers, firefighters, flight attendants, and mail carriers all have in common? They all wear **u**niforms! The clothes these workers wear make them easy to recognize. Some schools, too, ask that their students wear **u**niforms. And athletes often wear the **u**niform of their sports team. Next time you walk down the street, see how many different kinds of **u**niforms you can spot!

No one knows who invented the first **u**mbrella because **u**mbrellas have been around for about 3,000 years! Nowadays, we mainly use **u**mbrellas to keep off the rain. Originally, however, **u**mbrellas were used to block out the sun. In some cultures, the **u**mbrella was a symbol of power and wealth. In ancient Egypt, for example, only royalty and nobility were allowed to have **u**mbrellas. These important people had servants hold **u**mbrellas—often covered in leaves or feathers—over their heads to protect their faces from the sun.

To Read More

About the Letter U

Moncure, Jane Belk, and Helen Endres (illustrator). *Short "U" and Long "U" Play a Game.* Elgin, Ill.: The Child's World, 1979.

Noyed, Robert B. and Cynthia Klingel. *Cute! The Sound of Long U.* Chanhassen, Minn.: The Child's World, 2000.

About Uniforms

Williams, Barbara, and Sherry Meidell (illustrator). *ABC's of Uniforms and Outfits.* Nashville, Tenn.: Winston-Derek Publishers, 1992.

About Umbrellas

Josephson, Judith Pinkerton. *Umbrellas.* Minneapolis: Carolrhoda Books, 1998.

Liu, Jae Soo. *Yellow Umbrella.* La Jolla, Calif.: Kane/Miller Book Publishers, 2002.

Thaler, Mike, and Jerry Smath (illustrator). *Never Give a Fish an Umbrella and Other Silly Stories.* Mahwah, N.J.: Whistlestop, 1996.

Words with U

Words with U at the Beginning

ugly

Ulysses

umbrella

uncle

under

uniform

unsure

up

upstairs

Words with U in the Middle

about

chuckled

could

drummed

funny

guy

house

jumped

loud

out

outside

running

Russ

sound

sounds

suddenly

tutu

Words with U at the End

tutu

About the Authors

Cynthia Klingel has worked as a high school English teacher and an elementary teacher. She is currently the curriculum director for a Minnesota school district. Cynthia Klingel lives with her family in Mankato, Minnesota.

Robert B. Noyed started his career as a newspaper reporter. Since then, he has worked in communications and public relations for a Minnesota school district for more than fourteen years. Robert B. Noyed lives with his family in Brooklyn Center, Minnesota.